Hiba Hippo
Let's Rise Regardless Of Size!

An Artistic Children's Story About Body
Positivity And Self-Acceptance.

Written by: Stacy Shaneyfelt

Illustrated by: Hiba Abid

Dedication

In addition to my two extraordinary daughters, Kadena and Lucena, I also dedicate this book to my sweet and talented nieces and girl power superstars, Addison, Aria, Bri, Sophia, Isa, Briella, Gia, Caroline, Mia, Lily, and Aubrey. You're all beautiful, inside and outside, so let your personalities, hearts, and minds shine brightly.

To my amazing and empowering artist, friend, and collaborator, Hiba, I also devote this book to your resilience, beauty, intelligence, strength, and artistry!

Once upon a pool party in sunny Mozambique,

Hiba Hippo hides behind a capuluna so unique.

As the other cool animals dip, dive, and flip with glee,

She crouches like a mouse on her mammoth knees!

Like pink pearls of perfection, the flamingos gracefully pose.

In contrast, Hiba bawls like a baby, just honking her gigantic nose!

Hours later, she finally creeps to frolic and feast;

Secretly gobbling chocolate covered grass treats;

Hiba sighs, "Oh, how will I ever feel like the other stars?

My size is a big red flag, locking me in a tight jungle jar!"

Thinking hard, she's proud of her swimming and diving skills.

Water is her safe haven, granting Hiba lots of peace and thrills!

All at once, Hiba feels a poke
in her ballooning belly:

A sea turtle is giggling and
gurgling like a crazy ole jelly!

The turtle blows bubbles and
then greets her so politely,

"I'm Tito, nice to meet yo!" His
shell is painted brightly!

This frisky fellow is as wet as a whistle.

He's quite strange while chewing on thistle!

In turn, Hiba roars a loud and nervous grunt;

She aggressively splashes and gives him a punt!

But this calming critter just
chuckles and grins.

He's super cool and Zen, from
head to his fins!

Yet Hiba can't believe someone accepts her as she is.

Again, he paddles and persists with finesse and fizz...

Tito teases, "Sweet friend, there's no need to fret.

Just embrace yourself and let your body image jet!"

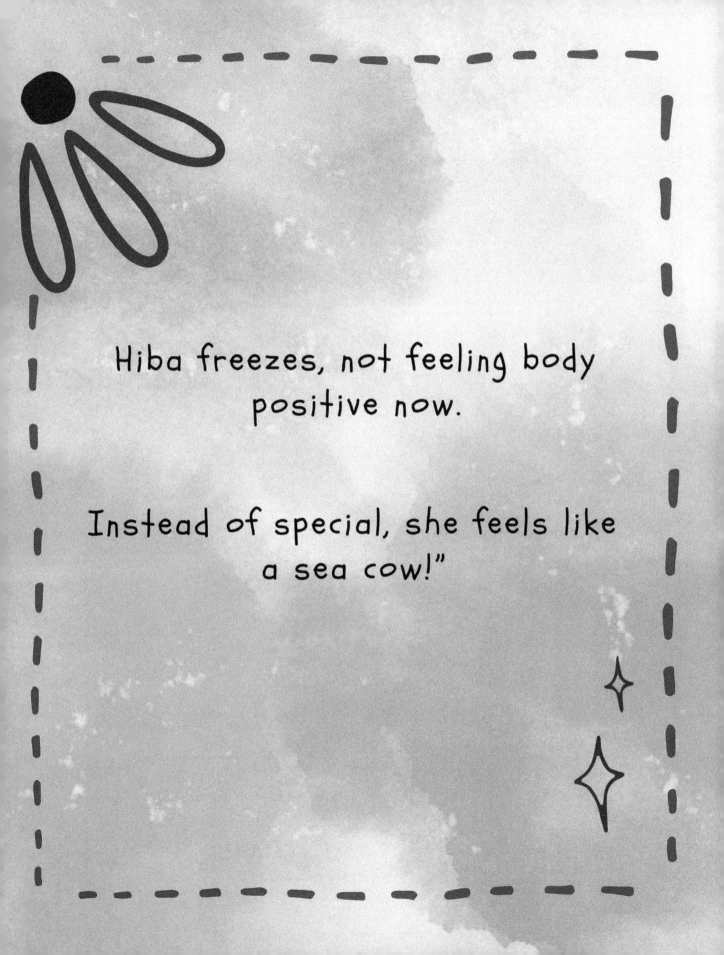

Hiba freezes, not feeling body
positive now.

Instead of special, she feels like
a sea cow!"

Hiba bellows, "Please stop your
perky pep talk?

I'm as wide as a barge. I wiggle
and jiggle when I walk!"

Again, Tito begs, "Chill your mind
and your body will follow.

Affirm positively with self-talk,
today, and tomorrow!"

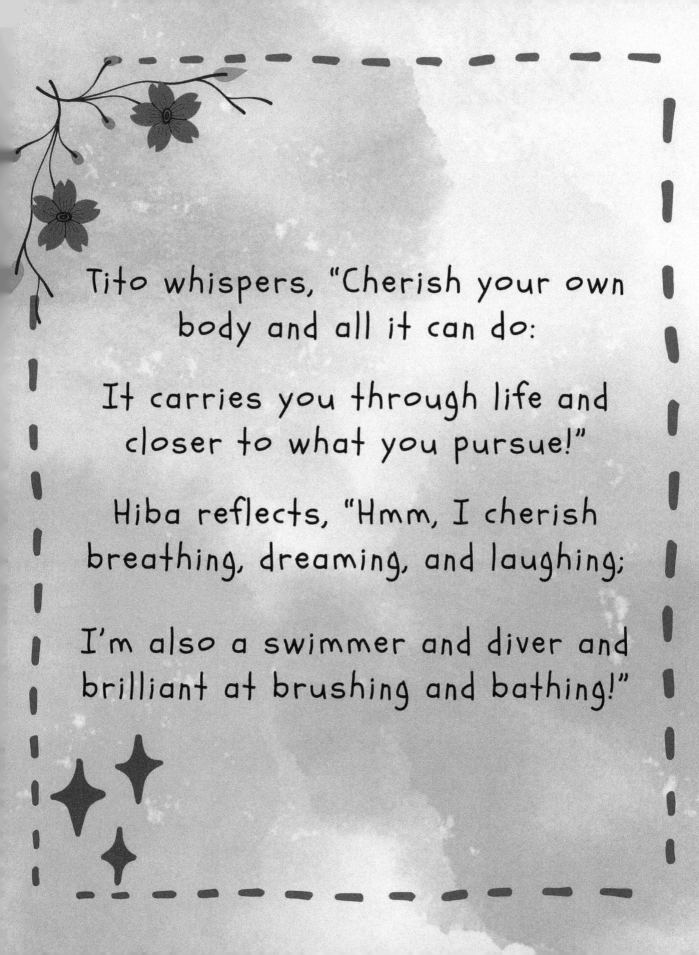

Tito whispers, "Cherish your own body and all it can do:

It carries you through life and closer to what you pursue!"

Hiba reflects, "Hmm, I cherish breathing, dreaming, and laughing;

I'm also a swimmer and diver and brilliant at brushing and bathing!"

Tito cheers, "See, keep a top 10 list of what you like about yourself the most:

Star the things unrelated to your weight or your favorite jams and toast!"

In turn, Hiba dives deep in her mind and excitedly scribbles a long list.

She exclaims, "My beauty isn't skin-deep!" A happy smile steals her lips.

When I feel good about myself, I show self-love, so unique!"

Tito gives her a high five because she's reaching her hippo peak!

Instantly, Tito reminds, "Beauty is a state of mind, not your outer looks-

Surround yourself with positive pals and use uplifting words, not hooks!"

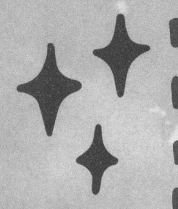

Hiba vows, I'll wear comfy clothes
that make me feel good.

"I'll sleep more and eat healthy to
fuel my body as I should!"

Following her promise, Hiba gleams
in her makeup art.

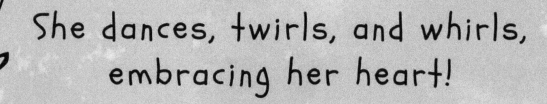

She dances, twirls, and whirls,
embracing her heart!

In the end, Hiba Hippo sings, "Let's rise regardless of size!"

Tito proclaims, "All bodies are gorgeous and diverse, not a curse!"

She agrees, "I trust my body and love myself as I am now!"

He concludes, "Be kind to your body and feel SO WOW!"

The End !

POST READING ACTIVITIES AND HAPPY HIPPO FUN

- <u>Happy Hippos:</u> Think like a scientist and go online with a grownup's permission to explore fun facts about hippos. You may also visit the local library to find 4-8 more exciting insights about them, their habitats, lifespans, sizes, diets, mannerisms, etc.

- <u>Rhyme on a Dime</u>: Based on the author's education and work history as a certified speech/drama teacher, she adds rhyme to give the story dramatic and musical flair. Locate 4-8 pairs of rhyming words. Practice reciting them aloud. Adding new rhymes to the sounds to make a fun game, perfect for a road trip, rainy day, vacation, or family fun night!

- <u>Rise Regardless of Size:</u> This book teaches a powerful life lesson and theme. Similarly, draw or doodle a picture, collage, or other piece to celebrate this theme. Be a rockin reader and art smart!

- <u>Terrific Tito:</u> In addition to hippos this book contains references to a sea turtle. Again, locate 4-8 fun science facts about one or more of these additional critters online with an adult's permission or from a local library book.

- <u>Word Wiz:</u> Enrich your vocabulary and spelling skills today. Jot down 4-8 new words from the book. For example, what does diverse mean? What about finesse? Go online with an adult's permission and define your new words. Lastly, use them in original sentences.

- <u>Book Blitz:</u> Imagine the author hires you to design a cover and title for the next book in the Hiba series. What will you call it? Which themes will be discussed? Will Tito be a part of this new book? Doodle or sketch your concept. Make art from the heart and love literacy!
- <u>Family Snack and Meal Menu</u>: Just as Hiba discovers healthy foods and mindful eating, make a healthy snack or meal menu for you and your loved ones this week. Get stealth health!
- <u>Character Acrostic</u>: Show your understanding of any of the characters' personalities. Create an acrostic poem using the character's name as your topic and inspiration. Polish your writing and spelling abilities!
- <u>Awesome Me</u>: Celebrate your inner and outer beauty by answering and affirming 4-5 of these mantras below. Practice body positivity now!

  1. My friends think I'm awesome because…
  2. My BFF says I'm wonderful at…
  3. I feel beautiful and strong when I…
  4. One unique thing about me is…
  5. I love who I am because…
  6. I rise at…
  7. I feel good about my…
  8. My family members admire me because…
- <u>Mirror, Mirror</u>: In order to feel better from the outside in, make a promise to spend less time in front of mirrors and selfie cameras, especially when they are making you feel uncomfortable and self-conscious about your body. Shine from within using body positivity!

THE AuTHoR

After obtaining her BS in Secondary English Education and MA in English from Slippery Rock University of PA, Stacy Shaneyfelt embarked on a successful teaching career that spanned public, government, and charter schools in Pittsburgh, PA, Oklahoma City, Norman, OK, and Okinawa, Japan. Stacy proudly earned a 2004 Fulbright-Hays Seminar Scholarship to Thailand and Vietnam from the United States Department of Education, Teacher of the Year in two schools, as well as other teaching accolades. However, her greatest achievements involved collaborating with other inspiring teachers and staff, meeting amazing families, and also interacting with memorable and diverse students who taught her so much about life and humanity!

In addition to multicultural and social activism, Stacy savors sweet moments with her awesome husband, two fierce and fabulous daughters, and three frisky fur babies. Stacy presently works as a virtual freelancer, private English and ESL tutor, online editor/proofreader, and blogger at https://www.upwork.com/fl/stacyshaneyfelt and www.brainmass.com. Stacy enjoys films, travel, books, coffee, art, and all things mindful!

THE ARTIST

Apart from pursuing her BS degree in Biotechnology from University of the Punjab, Lahore, Hiba embodies a passion of reflecting her heart, mind, and soul through the beautiful amalgam of colors. She strives to make her personality combination of Science and Art flourish each day. She truly believes in the cathartic power of "Art with HeART" and is embarked on a passionate journey to chase her artistic dreams.

In addition to her Art world, she is eager to explore the diversity and multiculturalism of the Real world. Recently, she has been honored as the Principal Candidate of the Fall 2021 Global UGRAD Culture Exchange program, hosted by Fulbright and USEFP, endowing her with a perfect opportunity to bridge the EAST (Pakistan) and the WEST (USA). This definitely marks an opening to a new chapter in the book of her life!

Hiba presently enjoys thriller books, sci-fi movies, adventurous trips, painting fantasies, and everything MAGICAL! She is currently a university student, Freelance Digital Illustrator, and also a Virtual Assistant for Stacy Shaneyfelt. Working for "Book Buzz" exemplifies yet again a new wonderful chapter in her life diary!

To discover more about her art, please visit https://www.instagram.com/hibacreates.png/

Thank you for buying this book. As a working mom and military spouse, your reviews mean so much to me because I aim to unite global readers through art and literacy. Kindly post a short review on this book's Amazon page. I truly appreciate this book buzz with me!

If you like this book, then please check out my other offerings at https://www.amazon.com/Stacy-Shaneyfelt/e/B08TVX7CSX

Love Yourself

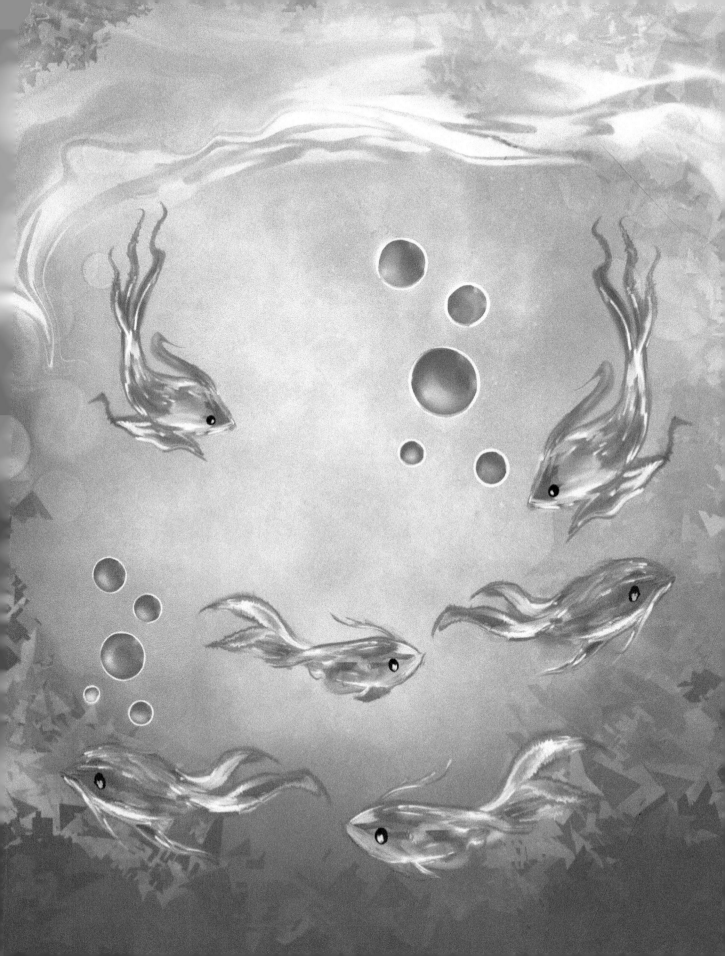